| DATE | | | |
|---|---|---|---|
|  |  |  |  |
|  |  |  |  |
|  |  |  |  |
|  |  |  |  |
|  |  |  |  |
|  |  |  |  |
|  |  |  |  |
|  |  |  |  |
|  |  |  |  |
|  |  |  |  |
|  |  |  |  |
|  |  |  |  |

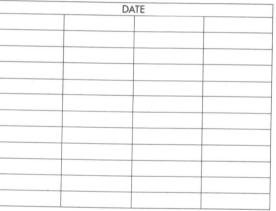

# As a tribute to the Senufo culture

Lord of the Dance
Copyright © 1988 by Véronique Tadjo
First published 1988 by A & C Black (Publishers) Ltd, London
For information address
J. B. Lippincott Junior Books, 10 East 53rd Street,
New York, N.Y. 10022.
Typography by Andrew Rhodes
1  2  3  4  5  6  7  8  9  10
First American Edition, 1989

Library of Congress Cataloging-in-Publication Data
Tadjo, Véronique, 1955-
    Lord of the dance.

    Summary: Poetically retells the story of the Senufo
people of Ivory Coast.
    [1. Senufo (African people)—Folklore.   2. Folklore—
Ivory Coast]   I. Title.
PZ8.1.T13Lo 1989        398.2'08996668 [E]        89-2785
ISBN 0-397-32351-4
ISBN 0-397-32352-2 (lib. bdg.)

*Acknowledgment*
The photograph of the Senufo artist is by Jean-Claude Nourault.

# Lord of the Dance

### an African retelling by

## Véronique Tadjo

J. B. Lippincott  New York

Once upon a time
There was the Mask
And he was living with
The sky and the earth

*Tom-tom-tom-tom-tom*

The Mask danced
With the moon
With the stars and the sun

*Tom-tom-tom-tom-tom*

And when the earth
Became our earth
When the valleys
The forests and the mountains
Sketched the horizon

When the water from the lakes
The rivers and the seas
Surrounded nature
And when the animals arrived
One by one

He came down
Among men and women
And together they danced

*Tom-tom-tom-tom-tom*

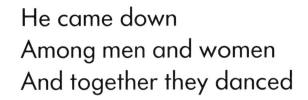

Sacred drums and rhythmic songs
To celebrate
Each joy and each happiness
But also to mourn
Each sadness and each suffering

*Tom-tom-tom-tom-tom*

And his voice rose:
Dance, dance, dance
I, the Mask,
Dance in the forest
To praise the gods
I dance in the village
To announce the next sowing
I dance to call the rains

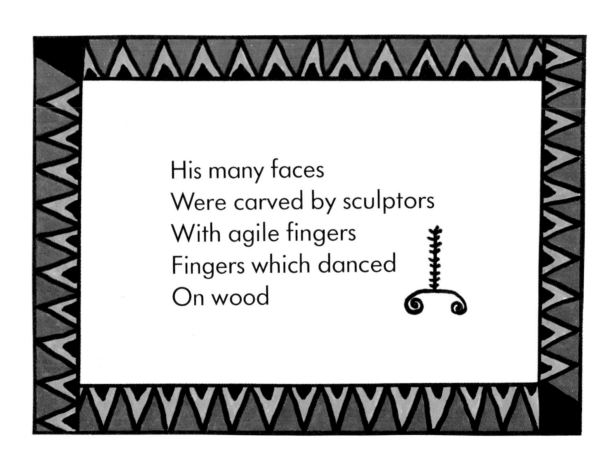

His many faces
Were carved by sculptors
With agile fingers
Fingers which danced
On wood

But one day
Somebody cried: Shame!
A mere piece of wood!
A symbol of ignorance!

And they put him away
And they hid him
And they sold him
In a city
Made of concrete and steel

But now they feel lonely
They remember the past
And they hear his voice:

*Tom-tom-tom-tom-tom*

I am the Mask
I still survive
I swirl like the wind
I leap like an antelope
I dance with farmers
With fishermen and hunters
I dance
In the popular quarters
Of African towns

*Tom-tom-tom-tom-tom*

I am
The spirit of the thunder
The spirit of the rainbow
The spirit of our fierce warriors
Of our ancestors—bearers of wisdom
The spirit of spirits

More beautiful than the moon on the lake
More powerful than the center of the earth

Child, let me tell you
A secret
Don't forget me
If you get lost
In the city
Or if you feel sad
Call me
And I shall guide your steps

*Tom-tom-tom-tom-tom*

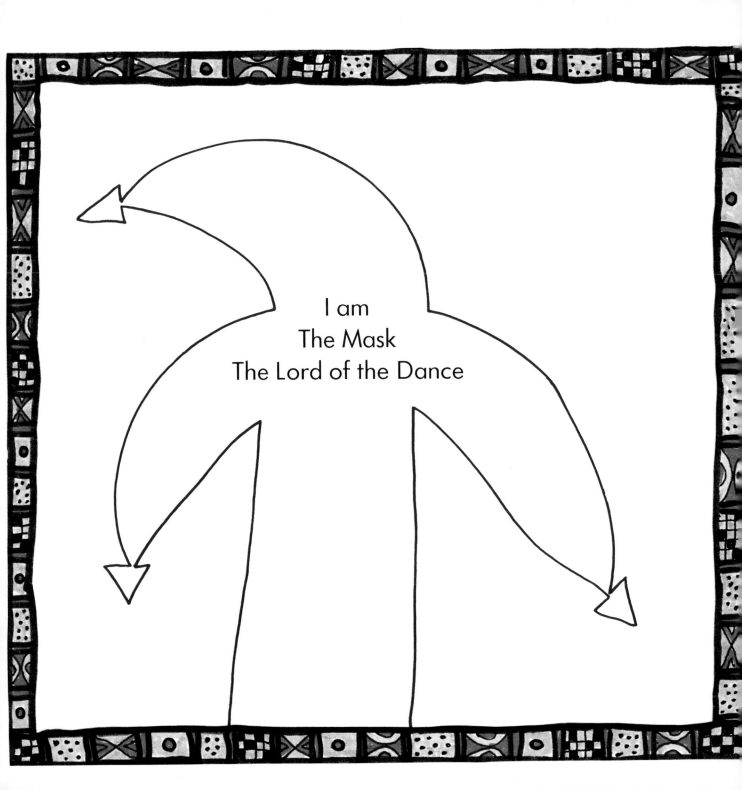

I am
The Mask
The Lord of the Dance

# Masks in the Côte d'Ivoire

In the north of the Côte d'Ivoire live the Senufo people. They are farmers and strongly believe in invisible spirits hidden in nature. The Senufo spin and weave their own cloth, which they decorate with pictures of these spirits as well as the characters and animals that are part of their daily life.

For ceremonies, Senufo spirits are represented by sacred masks, carved out of wood. There is a different mask for each spirit, so that just the right one can be brought out for a particular celebration or to express a particular feeling. Masks take the lead on occasions such as funerals and harvest festivals, for they can express both sorrow and rejoicing, both courage and fear.

A mask is worn only by a specially chosen person, who leads the villagers in their dance. There is music and singing to accompany the mask wherever it leads.

When a mask-carrier grows old and dies, a new person is chosen to wear the mask; and if the mask itself becomes damaged, it is repaired immediately, or a replacement carved. That is how these masks have survived to the present day, despite developments in the modern world that have forced other traditions to disappear. Even in the biggest African cities, you can still sometimes see people singing and dancing, led by a mask.

**Véronique Tadjo** is from the Côte d'Ivoire and spent three years teaching in the land of the Senufo people. During that time, she fell in love with their culture and became deeply interested in their way of life. She first heard "Lord of the Dance" sung at a wedding in England, and the hymn made her think of a Mask as Lord of the Dance for the Senufo in Africa.

Véronique Tadjo has illustrated her poem in the style of Senufo art, except that she has replaced the traditional brown vegetable ink with her own bright colors.